From his home on the other side of the moon, Father Time summoned eight of his most trusted storytellers to bring a message of hope to all children. Their mission was to spread magical tales throughout the world: tales that remind us that we all belong to one family, one world; that our hearts speak the same language, no matter where we live or how different we look or sound; and that we each have the right to be loved, to be nurtured, and to reach for a dream.

This is one of their stories.
Listen with your heart and share the magic.

FOR SYLVIE AND
HER UNCLE RICK,
WHOSE CAPACITY
TO LOVE HAS
AWAKENED OUR
HEARTS.

Our thanks to artists Shanna Grotenhuis, Jane Portaluppi, and Mindi Sarko,
as well as Sharon Beckett, Yoshie Brady, Andrea Cascardi, Solveig Chandler, Jun Deguchi,
Akiko Eguchi, Liz Gordon, Tetsuo Ishida, William Levy, Michael Lynton, Masaru Nakamura,
Steve Ouimet, Tomoko Sato, Isamu Senda, Minoru Shibuya, Jan Smith, and Hideaki Suda.

THE ELEPHANT PRINCE

Inspired by an Old Nordic Tale

Flavia Weedn & Lisa Weedn Gilbert

Illustrated by Flavia Weedn

Hodder Children's Books • Australia

Once upon a time, in the middle of a beautiful kingdom, there was a castle.

Now, this castle was very different from any other castle in the world, for it stood atop a tall glass hill, and sometimes at night, when the moon shone just right, it looked almost magical.

In the castle there lived a king and his beautiful princess daughter. The king loved his daughter with all his heart, but he was greatly troubled, for day by day the princess grew more and more unhappy and no one knew why. Because the princess kept her feelings to herself, even the king himself didn't know why she was so sad. Something was missing in the princess's life, and the king vowed to find her happiness.

So one day the king announced to all the townspeople that he would grant rule of half the kingdom and the princess's hand in marriage to the young man who could bring happiness to his daughter. But first the young man must climb to the top of the glass hill, where the princess would be waiting.

PROCLAMA

Hearye, h
hearye. E
known that
first young
who clim
glass hil
brings the
happines
give to h
half of the
and the
hand in m
T

PROCLAMATION

Hear ye, hear ye,
hear ye. Be it
known that to the
first young man
who climbs the
glass hill and
brings the princess
happiness, I will
give to him one
half of the kingdom
and the princess'
hand in marriage.
The King

Everyone in town knew that the path up the glass hill was as slick as ice and therefore almost impossible to climb unless one rode with the king in his royal coach.

So when, at last, the special day came, there were only three young men who were bold and brave enough to try.

The first was a jeweler's son who believed that more wealth would bring the princess true happiness. He cared little for the princess herself; it was only the rule of the kingdom he sought. He was certain that the mere sight of him on top of the glass hill, dressed in his long velvet coat and carrying satchels overflowing with jewels, would impress the princess, and for this he would win her hand and rule the kingdom.

The second was a farmer's son who also cared nothing for the princess, but he had dreams of becoming a brave and mighty knight. He thought that the sight of him in shining armor riding his magnificent horse up the glass hill would surely bring the princess happiness and win him the title of prince.

The third, the son of a poor family, had no jewels, no horse, no suit of armor. But he was kind and gentle and cared deeply about everything and everyone in the kingdom.

For years he had secretly loved the princess from afar and had wanted with all his heart to get a closer glimpse of her just to tell her how he felt. It was this wish, and this alone, that told him he, too, must try to climb the glass hill.

The day arrived, and all three men journeyed through the kingdom and into the village.

As they stood among the crowd the farmer's son said, "Only I, dressed as a knight, showing such bravery and magnificence, can impress the princess. Don't you see that? Only I will bring her happiness and win the title of prince."

But the jeweler's son said, "How very wrong you are! Nothing is as important as wealth and I am the wealthiest in the kingdom. It is I who will bring the princess happiness!"

Then they both began
to make fun of the poor
man's son, for it
was obvious to
them that he had
nothing of value
to offer the princess.
They laughed
at him and said,
"What have you
to bring the
princess?"

Hanging his head, the poor man's son told them he had only his heart and his love to offer the princess, and upon hearing this they threw back their heads and laughed even louder.

"Love!" they said. "That is all you have? What a fool you are! What has love to do with happiness? Even if you are able to climb the hill, the princess will surely laugh at you! You are a stupid man to even try."

The poor man's son was hurt by what they had
said but had little time to think about it, because
just then the trumpets sounded.
It was time for the jeweler's
son to begin his climb.

Confidently he began his journey, but halfway up the glass hill some jewels spilled from his satchel. As he reached to pick them up, he leaned over too far, and he and the jewels came tumbling all the way back down the hill.

Then the farmer's son mounted his horse, adjusted his armor, and began to climb.

He had just passed the halfway mark when he grew impatient and decided his horse was far too slow. With a mighty kick he commanded his horse to go faster, but in doing so the horse lost its footing and they both slid back down to the bottom of the glass hill.

It was time
for the poor
man's son to
make his try.

By now the
hill looked
steeper than
ever to him,
but he
gathered his
courage and
began to
climb.

When he was halfway up the hill, the poor man's son grew very tired and stopped to rest. He thought of the princess and wondered if she really would laugh at him because all he had to give her was his heart. Maybe the others were right after all. Maybe he shouldn't even try.

But then he remembered how much he loved the princess, and suddenly a magical thing happened. Just the thought of her gave him more strength and courage than he had ever imagined he could have. He took a deep breath and continued to climb until finally he was there. He had reached the top of the hill.

The princess had been watching him all along. Now, when she saw the pure love in his eyes, she realized that she loved him, too, and at that moment she gave him her heart.

Suddenly all her sadness disappeared as if by magic. And when the king saw this, he realized it was true love that had been missing from his daughter's life.

And so it was, on that day, that the king was given a special gift from his princess daughter: the gift of knowing that only true love can bring a heart true happiness.

With great pride, the king presented the new prince to the kingdom. And the trumpets sounded, telling the townspeople it was time to rejoice, for love would rule the kingdom forever.

That night there was a wonderful celebration, and magic filled the air. And from that time on, the prince and the princess lived and loved happily ever after, there in the castle that stood high atop the tall glass hill.

A Hodder Children's Book

Published in Australia and New Zealand in 1995
by Hodder Headline Australia Pty Limited,
(A member of the Hodder Headline Group)
10-16 South Street, Rydalmere NSW 2116

Produced in cooperation with Dream Maker Studios AG.

National Library of Australia Cataloguing-in-Publication data

Weedn, Flavia.
The elephant prince.

ISBN 0 7336 0026 3.

1. Fairy tales–Scandinavia. I. Gilbert, Lisa Weedn.
II. Title. (Series: Weedn, Flavia. Dream maker stories).

398.20948

The artwork for each picture is digitally mastered using acrylic on canvas.

Printed in Singapore